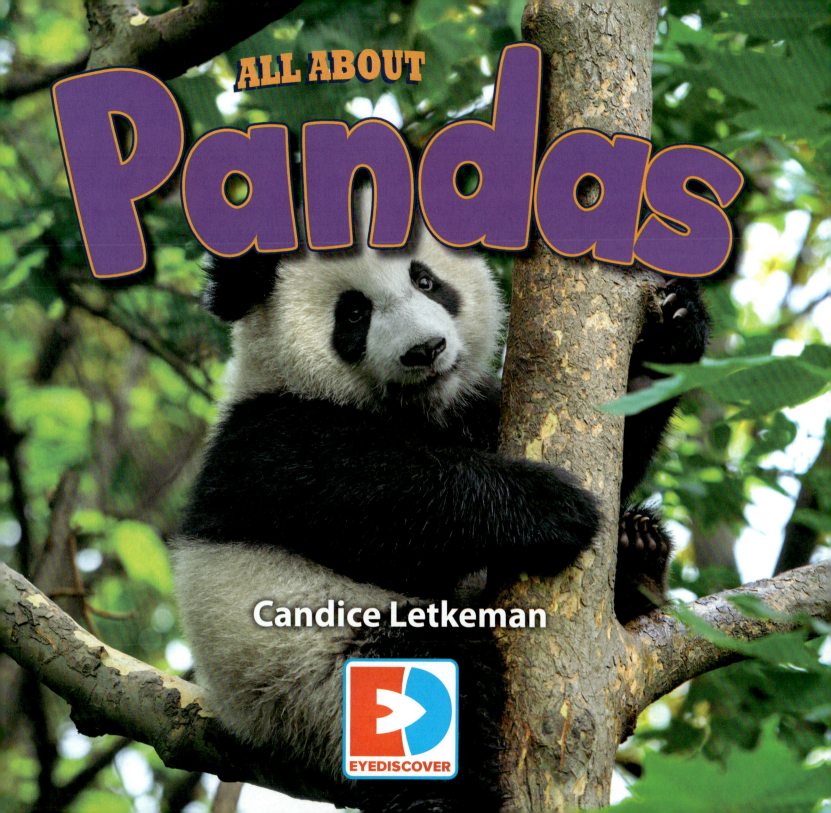

ALL ABOUT

Pandas

Candice Letkeman

EYEDISCOVER

EYEDISCOVER

Go to **www.eyediscover.com** and enter this book's unique code.

BOOK CODE

E466296

EYEDISCOVER brings you optic readalongs that support active learning.

Published by AV² by Weigl
350 5th Avenue, 59th Floor New York, NY 10118
Website: www.eyediscover.com

Library of Congress Control Number: 2017930719

ISBN 978-1-4896-5674-2 (hardcover)

Printed in the United States of America
in Brainerd, Minnesota
1 2 3 4 5 6 7 8 9 0 21 20 19 18 17

072017
020317

Editor: Katie Gillespie
Designer: Mandy Christiansen

Weigl acknowledges Getty Images, iStock, Minden, and Shutterstock as the primary image suppliers for this title.

EYEDISCOVER provides enriched content, optimized for tablet use, that supplements and complements this book. EYEDISCOVER books strive to create inspired learning and engage young minds in a total learning experience.

I am a lion.

Watch
Video content brings each page to life.

Browse
Thumbnails make navigation simple.

Read
Follow along with text on the screen.

Listen
Hear each page read aloud.

Your EYEDISCOVER Optic Readalongs come alive with...

Audio
Listen to the entire book read aloud.

Video
High resolution videos turn each spread into an optic readalong.

OPTIMIZED FOR

☑ **TABLETS**

☑ **WHITEBOARDS**

☑ **COMPUTERS**

☑ **AND MUCH MORE!**

ALL ABOUT
Pandas

In this book, you will learn about

- **how they look**

- **where they live**

- **what they eat**

and much more!

Pandas are mammals. They have round faces, and thick black and white coats.

5

Pandas live in bamboo forests in China.

Pandas like to be by themselves.

Pandas are good at climbing trees. They like to sleep in trees sometimes.

Pandas are curious and playful. They can roll and do somersaults.

Baby pandas are called cubs. Mother pandas usually have only one cub at a time.

15

Pandas eat bamboo. They sit up to eat and hold the bamboo in their front paws.

16

Pandas are one of the rarest animals on Earth. There are not many of them left in nature.

Pandas need bamboo forests to stay happy and healthy. People can help pandas by taking care of the planet.

PANDAS BY THE NUMBERS

Pandas **grow** to be **6 feet long**.
(1.8 meters)

There are **fewer** than **2,000 pandas** in the world today.

Pandas **can run** **11** **miles per hour**.
(18 kilometers per hour)

Pandas eat more than **30 pounds** of bamboo **each day.**

(13.6 kilograms)

Pandas **weigh** more than **220 pounds.**

(100 kg)

Pandas live for about **20 years.**

KEY WORDS

Research has shown that as much as 65 percent of all written material published in English is made up of 300 words. These 300 words cannot be taught using pictures or learned by sounding them out. They must be recognized by sight. This book contains 39 common sight words to help young readers improve their reading fluency and comprehension. This book also teaches young readers several important content words, such as proper nouns. These words are paired with pictures to aid in learning and improve understanding.

Page	Sight Words First Appearance
5	and, are, faces, have, they, white
7	in, live
8	be, by, like, to
11	at, good, sometimes, trees
12	can, do
15	a, mother, one, only, time
16	eat, the, their, up
19	animals, Earth, left, many, not, of, on, them, there
20	help, need, people

Page	Content Words First Appearance
5	coats, mammals, pandas
7	bamboo forests, China
8	themselves
12	somersaults
15	cubs
16	paws
19	nature
20	planet

Watch
Video content brings each page to life.

Browse
Thumbnails make navigation simple.

Read
Follow along with text on the screen.

Listen
Hear each page read aloud.

I am a lion.

EYEDISCOVER

Go to www.eyediscover.com and enter this book's unique code.

BOOK CODE

E466296